BIG**FAT**

Threesome

Hedonist

Hedonist

CONTENTS

BIG FAT THREESOME

"Dude. I think I love her."

Those seemingly innocent words, spoken by one of my two favourite people in the whole world, stop me in my tracks. I peep around the corner and observe Daniel and Josh from behind. They're sitting on the large couch in front of the TV, X-Box controllers in hand. Their fleshy backs are turned towards me, but I can still make out how both of their t-shirts are straining to contain their big, sexy bodies. These two have really grown into their own ever since I moved into this flat share and started cooking for them. One is even more delicious than the other.

"The fuck, man," Josh says, while putting his controller down and turning to Dan.

"I'm serious!" the latter argues.

"Yeah, it's just… Me too."

They share a silent look. I forget to breathe. I could swear my heart is beating so loudly, they should be able to hear it from all the way over there.

"Well then," Daniel says. "I suppose at least one of us is going to end up disappointed."

I bite my bottom lip.

"Or more likely, both of us. I mean, just look at her. She's a solid ten in my book. And we're… She's not going to be interested," Josh mumbles. "That's why I've been keeping it to myself. Plus, we vowed that we'd never let a girl come between us."

"Yeah, I guess you're right. It's hopeless, isn't it?"

They each let out a dejected sigh and then turn to face the TV again.

No fucking way!

Shaken, I head back into the kitchen to check on the roasted chicken in the oven, and the potatoes boiling away on the stove. My concentration is all over the place. I can't forget what I just walked in on. Words that were never meant for my ears, and yet… God how I wish I could hear them again, directed at me this time.

They're in love with me. *Both of them.*

I feel faint, and ecstatic, and I don't know what else. Because, of course I love them too. *Both of them.*

Josh and Dan have been amazing roommates. In the sense that they're easy-going and super chill to live with. They're always up for a good time and a great meal. They've been entirely willing--even enthusiastic subjects in the little experiment I've been conducting in our shared home. As much food as I've made, they've been all too eager to polish it off. As a result, they've been getting bigger and sexier by the day. And I've been having a hard time keeping my attraction under control. The only reason I haven't tried to seduce either of them is because I was terrified it would ruin the great dynamic we already shared.

When I first moved in, they were already on the chubby side, but not unusually so. Still, it was obvious that they enjoyed their food and I was smitten already. There was just one problem: neither of them could cook and they didn't have a whole lot of money either.

So, after I answered their ad for a third roommate, and they got over the initial shock that I was in fact female, I quickly determined that their meals had consisted largely of frozen stuff from the supermarket and takeout.

They didn't seem to want a girl to move in initially. I guess because as they said, they were not going to let a woman come in between their friendship. But as soon as I offered to cook… Well, they were sold on that idea pretty much immediately, and so was I.

I moved in my stuff the very next day. And it began.

Home cooked meals every day, plus cakes and desserts and anything else they could possibly ask for. I prepared it; they ate it. And their hunger for my food has been absolutely insatiable. As a feeder, this satisfied me beyond belief.

Little did I know that while I watched them eat, and obsessed about every pound their growing bodies added on, they had noticed me too. All the nights I've spent, fantasising about what it would be like to do more than just *feed them*… All those times I fingered myself while thinking about how much fatter they'd grown since I moved in. Josh and Daniel have both put on at least eighty pounds each. If not more. Probably more. They've got to be pushing 350 or 400lbs by now. Sadly, we don't have a scale strong enough to weight them…

None of their clothes fit properly anymore. They've stopped trying to squeeze into their jeans and can mostly be found in sweat pants or shorts on most days. All of their t-shirts, even the ones that started off super baggy, have become tight, much to my delight.

They're saving up for some new stuff, but with most of the monthly budget being spent on food, there isn't much left. And I'm certainly not complaining, because the tighter their clothes get, the more of an eyeful I get every time I look at them.

And they've been glorious to behold.

Josh, with his strawberry blonde hair and blue eyes, looks a bit like a fat angel now. His face has become rounder over the last few months. There's a bit of a double chin developing. I have to fight the urge to touch his gorgeous chubby face multiple times a day. And his body, oh my! Soft and squishy all over; with pronounced moobs and wobbly love handles that jiggle and shake with every step when he walks.

Then there's Daniel. *Tall, dark and handsome*, as I like to call him in my dreams. Dark skin, black hair and full kissable lips to complement his expressive dark brown eyes. His body is a little different; he carries a lot of weight around his hips and ass. On top of that he has grown quite a substantial belly by now, thanks to my thrice-daily feedings. I've never been with a black guy before, so that in itself would have been enough to get me interested.

I'd liked them both the second we first met, but now, I *know* them. And my superficial lust has been replaced with something much deeper and more insidious. I want to possess them. I selfishly want them all to myself. Why shouldn't I? After all, I'm responsible for every additional ounce of fat they've gained. All this sexiness, I helped *create* it!

Sadly, I've been too cowardly to act on it, or even to hint at my feelings. If they knew how utterly obsessed I have become, they might pull away, or so I thought. They might throw me out and never look back. Because I'm quite the freak, deep down.

To think that it might be mutual is driving me absolutely crazy now. I can't even imagine how *they* feel. I mean, for two guys to actually share emotions that deep… it had to be eating away at them until now, right? And now what? They're not going to expect me to choose, are they? I wouldn't know how. Can't we all just get along?

I'm still mindlessly chewing my bottom lip while checking the roast chicken's internal temperature with a meat thermometer. Ready, time to take it out.

There's no way out. My days of hiding in the kitchen, obsessing about my two chubby roommates in silence, are over. I'm going to have to make a move somehow, because it's clear that they've already given up. I must let them know that I feel the same way about them. I need a plan, to get my message across loud and clear.

But please, oh please! Don't make me choose!

Lunch has been served, and so, my work in the kitchen is done for now. I serve half a chicken each to Dan and Josh, along with a generous helping of creamy mashed potato doused in rich gravy. They're excited, and so am I.

I never realised just how satisfying it could be to cook for people, as long as they're willing like these two. Not before I moved in here and explored this side of my sexuality.

But I only stand and watch them for a little while as they eat, because I have a plan to put into motion. A plan that is going to make our little arrangement all the more satisfying, I hope.

It's difficult, tearing myself away from the sight of the two of them eagerly shovelling food into their mouths, pausing only briefly to compliment me. How much has changed today.

Now, when I feel their eyes on me, my heart jumps all the more. Because I know I'm not just their roommate anymore. I'm being desired for more than just my cooking skills.

And that's precisely why I can no longer accept the status quo.

I slip away from my beautiful hungry boys to freshen up. No more sweats and baggy t-shirt. It's a beautiful afternoon outside - first of the season- so I'm going all out to get a rise out of them.

I change into a bright red bikini and wrap-around skirt. Brush my hair a little. Apply some lip gloss and mascara. Armed with a towel, and a book, I march past them into the kitchen and grab a bottle of beer from the fridge.

"Bon Appetit, you guys. It's so nice out, I'm going to sunbathe for a while," I say, while passing the small round dining table back towards the balcony doors that lead off from the lounge.

Earlier, the clanging of cutlery had filled the air, but now… silence.

I glance back at them, only to find two pairs of hungry eyes fixated on me. They're so perfect; my two men of the house. They're both sitting wide-legged on their chairs to accommodate their big bellies, growing tauter as they fill up on chicken and mash. Fleshy thighs stick out from their slightly ill-fitting shorts. Thick arms poke out from the too-tight sleeves of their t-shirts to lean down on the solid wooden table. I love how small they make that table look. How small they'd make me feel if only I could get what I want from them. *Both of them.*

"Uhh, okay," Josh stammers.

"Thanks for lunch," Daniel says.

I smile sweetly at the two of them and turn around again to open the door. The patio furniture outside has seen better days, but I'm not going to let that bother me. Instead, I cover the most comfortable one of the mismatched grouping of chairs with my towel and arrange another one to serve as an extension to rest my legs on. Then, I take the sarong off.

I hope they're watching through the window.

I take a swig of beer and enjoy how the cold liquid

passes down my throat. It *is* a wonderful day. Clear blue skies, bright sunshine, and the unmistakable perfume of summer flowers in the air. It's impossible not to feel cheerful when the weather is this nice. Winter is finally over.

I sit back and sigh deeply, closing my eyes. I wish I'd remembered to wear some sunglasses before coming out here. Oh well, perhaps I'll ask one of them to fetch them from my room.

Along with the sun screen, which I purposely left in my underwear drawer.

It's all part of the game.

For a few minutes, I just sit there, collecting my thoughts, planning my next move and downing that bottle of beer for courage. I think again about what they said. And I wonder whether their feelings towards me are entirely pure, or as filthy and depraved as mine are.

I hope it's the latter, or my plan might fail miserably yet.

Because what I need from the two of them isn't puppy love. I'm not pure of heart; I'm a deviant. If they're going to give me what I *really* want, they're going to have to get down and dirty.

I pull out my phone and idly scroll through my newsfeed, when another idea occurs to me. After switching the phone to selfie mode, I try to make a sexy pose. It's not something I'm good at, but a few tries later, I finally get a picture slutty enough to work for my purposes. I share it in our roommates WhatsApp group. With the camera still on, I angle the screen in such a way to give me a view of the table through the large windows. Sure enough, Josh picks up his phone and checks the notification. I wish I could see his expression up close, but even from here it's obvious that he's thoroughly got the message.

I swiftly open up the group chat and type a hurried message to fuck with them a little.

"Oh crap you guys, wrong chat window."

Now even Daniel has his phone out, and the two of them are starting to argue back and forth. Are they wondering who I meant to send that to? Are they getting jealous perhaps?

I can see that Josh is typing something, but the message never arrives in the group chat. Maybe that was cruel. I bite my lip to try and contain all these nerves and butterflies. Flirting is hard, dammit! But I can't rely on my cooking skills forever, can I? Complacency is no longer an option.

All this time, I've held back and tried to ignore my feelings. And what have I got in return? I've driven myself even crazier with desire. Because while they're growing bigger and more beautiful by the day, they've never once made a pass at me. There hasn't been a hint of innuendo. No teasing. No flirtations. They thought I wouldn't be interested, because they've gained some weight. *As if!*

I start typing again.

"Oh, would someone mind fetching my sunscreen? I forgot it in my room."

If this doesn't send the right message, I don't know

what will.

I check the reflection in the screen and see that Daniel has gotten up from the table and disappeared, probably into my room. Yep, a response arrives soon after.

"Where is it?" Daniel writes.

"Top drawer of my dresser."

I wait with bated breath. Dammit. I really wish I could see his face while he's going through my bras and panties to find it. If I'd had more time to plan this, I should have planted a camera in there.

By now, curiosity seems to have gotten the better of Josh, because he's also getting up. God, he's sexy. They both are. As they've grown over the winter, their walks have changed a bit. Slower, more deliberate, with a certain sway and gravitas only a large man can have. I don't know why I like that, but I do. Every step they take, I imagine what it would feel like to be sandwiched between the two of them.

Maybe soon, I'll get to live out that fantasy. *Hopefully even today*! If all goes well...

The balcony door creaks behind me and Daniel appears with the bottle of sunscreen. He looks bashful; won't make eye contact with me while he hands it to me. I think I catch him looking at my ample cleavage a few times. This bikini doesn't leave much to the imagination... I wonder what's going on inside his head now? Is it the same that's going on in mine? Is it only love he feels or is there a healthy dose of lust as well? I hope so, because for me the two are inextricably linked.

"Thanks, Dan. You're so sweet," I say. "Have you guys finished the chicken?"

He nods. "Yeah."

"I got ice cream for dessert. It's so nice out, why don't you get the tub and we can all have it out here?" I suggest.

He glances at the two remaining chairs out of the mismatched set of four and nods. "Okay."

"Something wrong? You seem off today," I remark.

"Nah, nothing. Just tired, I guess."

I smile at him. "Perfect time to sit and chill in the sun, then. Tell Josh also."

I watch as he turns away from me and heads back inside. God, he must be really jealous of the imaginary guy I was pretending to send that selfie to.

Through the window, I can see him talking to Josh and pointing out at the balcony. The latter nods and grabs a few bowls from the kitchen. Daniel gets the ice cream out of the freezer. Wonderful. My plan is coming together.

By the time they reach me, they're both looking quite glum. Their sullen expressions tear at my heartstrings. Hopefully we can find a way for all of us to be happy, and soon.

Josh hands me a bowl and a spoon.

"Thanks." I smile at him, but he doesn't smile back.

God, it was only a bit of fun! I wanted to rile them up; make them want to compete for me, but all I've managed to do is hurt their feelings.

Daniel serves me a large scoop of ice cream first and

wants to add another, but I stop him.

"That's plenty for me. I basically got it for you guys. I know how much you enjoy your double chocolate chip," I say.

"Okay."

Again, it's obvious that he's upset. It's surprising just how much that affects me. Guilt is setting in. It would be so much easier if either of them had confessed their feelings to *me*, rather than to each other. But there's no way that's going to happen now. I'm digging a hole for myself, and I'm going to have to get us all out of it again.

I put my bowl of ice cream down in my lap and a shiver passes through me as the cold penetrates my skin. I can feel my nipples harden as a result. Hopefully the boys are looking.

I eat a few spoonfuls. Slowly. Deliberately. Does it look seductive? I hope so...

Once I've finished my dessert, I open the sunscreen and squeeze a dollop of it into my palm. I start spreading it around on my legs, starting at the calf and working my way up to my thighs, all the way to the edge of the bikini bottom.

My audience has been captivated. Both Josh and Daniel try not to stare, but fail miserably. Their movements slow, like they've all but forgotten about the large helpings of ice cream melting away in their hands. Four eyes burn into me, exciting me, making me crave their attention even more.

They keep looking at me, heightening all my senses.

My skin prickles with excitement as I try to work the lotion into it with slow, circular movements.

Once I'm done massaging my legs and taking a whole lot more time than strictly necessary, I move on to my midriff. Then my arms, shoulders, and finally, my cleavage, even dipping the tips of my fingers in underneath the bikini to make sure I don't miss a spot.

It's so silent out here, you could hear a pin drop. It seems they're even holding their breaths now. Can they hear my heart race? I can. It's rushing in my ears.

"I can't quite reach my back properly," I remark, looking up at them.

Josh has turned bright red; from his cheeks all the way to his ears. As for Daniel… little beads of sweat are starting to collect on his brow. Their expressions are tense; their eyes wide.

Josh clears his throat. "It's warm out here."

I smile at him. "Yeah, so nice, isn't it?"

Although they obviously heard me the first time, neither of them seems willing to step up. But I'm desperate to close this gap between us. Can they not see how much I yearn to be touched?

I hold up the sun lotion bottle. "My back, please? I don't want a sunburn."

"Erm, right," Daniel says, while scooting his chair closer.

Now I'm the one trying not to stare. Do my eyes deceive me or is he sporting quite a substantial bulge in his shorts right now? Instinctively, I lick my lips.

Oh god, these boys are killing me.

I glance at Josh, who still looks pretty flustered. His arms are folded in his lap, as though he's trying to hide a bodily reaction of his own. It's making me squirm just thinking about it. Two big men, with shorts full of wood. I swear to God I'll lose my mind if I don't get to take this thing to the next level, and soon!

Daniel takes the bottle from me and squirts just a bit too much sunscreen into his hand. The sound of it as he rubs his hands together is positively filthy. I tremble with anticipation and lean forward to give him access to my back. Josh is staring at the eyeful of propped up cleavage he's getting now. He's not even trying to hide it anymore.

As soon as Dan's hand touches my back, my body reacts; as does my heart. The thumping in my throat makes me light headed.

"Thanks, that feels really good," I mumble.

Josh inhales sharply while he carries on watching us. His right hand twitches, as though he's desperate to do something about the growing situation in his shorts. Meanwhile, Daniel's touch becomes more insistent and confident, as he carries on rubbing the excess lotion into the skin on my back.

"If I knew you were this good at giving backrubs, I might have asked for one sooner," I remark, while turning over to study his face.

His lips twitch, but he doesn't say anything. His expression doesn't calm in the slightest. Oh, he's struggling for control, alright!

I look at Josh again.

"Say… Aren't you tempted to do a bit of sunbathing as well?" I ask.

He barely even looks up. "Isn't that what we're doing?"

"I mean… with your shirt off," I say. "The sun screen is already here. I could help you apply it."

Am I being too forward? Despite all the time spent in close quarters these last few months, I haven't had the chance to see either of them topless. Come to think of it, they've been pretty fucking shy. Always keeping their doors closed. Always fully changed before leaving the bathroom after a shower… I'm desperate to see just where all my cooking has ended up. Desperate to *touch* it…

"Nah, that's okay," Josh says. "I'm quite comfortable as is."

He doesn't look comfortable, though. And I guess the disappointment is written on my face too, because he gives me a strange look. "How about you, Daniel?" I turn to face him, marvelling at his gorgeous face, so close to my shoulder.

Our eyes meet, and I get so faint I forget to breathe. He smells delicious; always does. Whatever cologne he uses, it's bloody amazing.

"What?" he asks; no, he breathes. His voice has gone hoarse all of a sudden.

Jesus, can't they tell what I'm trying to do here? Are they really so clueless?

If I can see so clearly how much they're struggling

right now, why can't they see the same in me?

"I was wondering if maybe *you* wanted to take your shirt off. The sun feels *so good.*"

He presses his lips together while he stares at mine.

"Or perhaps you'd want to-" I whisper.

"I'd want to, what?"

Ugh, they're both being wilfully dense. I can't take it anymore.

"Dammit, that picture was meant for you guys!" I blurt out. "Now what are you going to do about it?"

He looks shocked, like I just slapped him in the face rather than confessed my intentions. I glance over at Josh, who is awkwardly running his hand through his hair while exhaling sharply.

Daniel straightens himself in his chair. With his hands no longer on my shoulders, I feel strangely naked and vulnerable. That could have gone a whole lot better. *Stupid!*

"What are you trying to say?" he asks.

It takes everything I've got not to backtrack now. It's confession time. "I really like you," I whisper, while overtly staring at his lips. Then I look over at Josh again. "Both of you."

"We like you too," Josh admits. Hearing him say these words in my presence this time unleashes a whole swarm of butterflies in my chest.

"Right," I say. "But the thing is-"

"Tell me," Daniel urges.

"I wouldn't know how to choose." I fold my arms, then unfold them again. Fuck, why does it have to be this hard just to be honest? "So, I was rather hoping you wouldn't make me."

"You're joking, right?" Daniel asks.

"I can't believe this," Josh mumbles.

I shake my head and press my lips together. "I'm dead serious. It's why I wanted to move in. Why do you think I volunteered to take care of you guys? I so badly want to see you happy, and I just didn't know how else to do it. So, I've been feeding you ever since. And you seemed to enjoy my food, so I kept on making more of it. But I'd like more than that..."

Josh laughs awkwardly while running his hand over his chin now. I can't stop myself from overtly staring at his crotch now. He's definitely still hard. I so wish I could see him in his full glory.

"So, what do you think?" I ask, my voice so flat I can hardly hear myself over the blood rushing in my ears.

I wait with bated breath while Daniel and Josh exchange a flustered look, and then focus their eyes back on me again.

"You're not joking, right?" Daniel asks again.

I shake my head. "I swear."

"It's better than the alternative," Daniel mumbles.

"Jesus Christ," Josh says.

I'm so aroused. So nervous, yet so ecstatic. And yet *nothing* is happening. Nobody is getting up. Nobody is taking my hand, touching me, holding me. *Nothing.*

"Will one of you make a move already, please? I'm going crazy over here!" I plead.

Daniel, who was already right beside me, is the first

to approach. With one arm wrapped around my waist, he presses his lips into mine. It's the most beautiful feeling, to be claimed by one of them for the first time.

His shuddering breaths tickle my face, while he carefully teases my lips open. There's so much tension inside my chest, I can't suppress a moan when my tongue touches his for the first time.

When I open my eyes and look at him, I can see the desperation written on his face. His kisses become firmer, more urgent. I glance over at Josh, whose cheeks have become even redder by now. I wave at him to come closer. He stumbles out of the chair and hesitates. I reach for his hand and coax him towards me the rest of the way.

"Please," I whimper against Daniel's lips, who pulls back just enough for me to turn my attention to Josh. "Kiss me?" I beg.

Josh leans down, causing ripples to form all over his soft squishy belly. I wrap my arm around his neck and tenderly kiss his lips for the first time.

Fireworks erupt in my chest when I get a taste of his sweet tongue. I look up into his eyes and find that they are getting just a bit moist. It's heart wrenching to see what an effect I'm having on either of them. I hope they can see how deeply they're affecting me too.

Such a beautiful moment; perfect in every way.

Finally, I'm finding out whether all those wet dreams I've had come close to reality or not. They really don't. This moment right here, it's so much sexier, so much more beautiful than I could have ever imagined.

"We should go inside," I breathe, in between nibbles of Josh's bottom lip. "Get some privacy."

Daniel nods and pushes his chair back. Josh, of course, is already up on the other side of me and ready to go. I kick the chair away from my feet and get up, wrapping my left arm around Dan's neck, and my right around Josh's waist.

How beautiful they both are. Just perfect. I pull them in tighter, until I can feel their big bodies pressing into me from either side. It drives me wild to have them this close to me. By now, I'm so wet, it's soaking into my bikini bottom.

"I can't believe this," Josh mumbles. Daniel doesn't say anything.

Glancing down towards my left and right, it's obvious they're both rocking quite substantial wood for me. Good; that's exactly what I crave.

I'm a pleaser; always have been. So far, I've been trying to satisfy them with copious amounts of home cooking, but now I'm going to do so much more than that. I'm going to make sure Josh and Dan are fully sated in every possible way today. That's how I'll get my own release. Because I do love them. *Both of them.*

Daniel leads the way inside, and I take a moment to appreciate that nice, round ass of his. Would it be too weird if I gave him a little whack? I decide not to, just yet, and glance back at Josh, who is following behind me. His fingers are hooked into mine, and he's got a look in his eyes which I've never seen before. A kind of hunger, but not for food this time. It matches my own.

"My room," I say, causing Dan to speed up just a little ahead of me. His impatience makes me smile.

When I bought my new bed, especially for this place, I'd been hoping for exactly this. As a result, it's the only king sized one in the house. The three of us are going to need the space.

Daniel pushes the door open so hard; it bounces against the stopper in the wall.

Josh, on the other hand, is a much gentler soul. He closes it carefully, then just stands there, staring at me.

"Are you sure?" he mumbles. "You really want this? I mean..."

I smile briefly and nod. "A hundred percent."

Daniel takes my hand and leads me to the bed, before cupping my face and planting his lips against mine again. He's obviously the more confident one out of the two, just as I'd expected. If this is going to work out, I'll have to make sure to coax Josh along too, or he'll feel left out.

I push Dan back and smile at him. "Not so fast, Romeo. Take your shirt off for me first."

Then, I turn to Josh and gesture at him to come closer, then take his beautiful chubby face into my hands and kiss him deeply again. He groans into my lips as his big fat body shudders into me. The bulge in his shorts has only grown since I first spotted it. I run my hand down his chest, over his sexy soft belly and cup my hand over his erection.

He moans loudly; only quieting when I kiss him with renewed vigour. His sweet tongue sends shivers down my spine. He's so eager. So ready to surrender himself to me. I simply adore him.

Daniel moves in next to me; he's a glorious sight with his top off. Dark, flawless skin as far as the eye can see. Just a few short black curls adorn his chest right in the middle of his chubby man tits, and run down along the centre of his round belly. He's absolutely gorgeous in his own way. Better than my wildest dreams could have foretold. I cop a feel of his crotch too, causing him to grind and shudder into my hand.

"You're so big!" I squeal.

I back away from the two of them, and pull the strings at the back of my bikini top until it falls down. No longer do they have to undress me with their eyes; I'm almost fully on display for them.

"Jesus fucking Christ," Daniel mutters.

Josh seems stunned into silence.

I get up onto the mattress and lie back, leaning on my elbows.

"Come join me," I say.

Further encouragement is unnecessary. They both move in simultaneously, crawling onto the bed on either side of me. The mattress wobbles and shifts underneath them, and the bed creaks dangerously. Luckily, it holds.

Josh touches me first. It begins with one careful caress along my side, travelling upwards but pausing at the swell of my left boob. His breathing has sped up; he's really struggling to stay calm now.

Daniel gets onto all fours on my right and leans down to kiss the side of my neck. It's a beautiful gesture that gives me goose bumps all over.

I turn to look at Josh, who seems to be frozen in place beside me. I don't quite recognise the look in his eyes, and he won't look at me straight.

"God, Lucy. You're so hot," Daniel moans, while continuing to kiss his way down my neck towards my shoulder. It's perfect, except…

Josh is shaking his head now. "No. This is wrong."

"Josh!" I call out, and put my hand over his. It's clammy. He pulls it away.

"We promised we wouldn't let a girl come in between us. I intend to keep that promise. For everyone's sake, I'm out." His face is still bright red, his eyes glazed over, and his expression tense. He retreats faster than I've ever seen him move, leaving Dan and me alone in my bed.

"Fuck," I complain. My heart has sunk into my stomach. I feel as though I'm falling, with nothing and no one to catch me. Have I just fucked everything up? Everything was just perfect, and now… Josh's departure hurts like nothing I've ever felt before.

Dan looks up from my cleavage. "Am I doing it wrong?"

"It's Josh. I think he's upset," I say. My throat feels tight and my heart is going crazy. This isn't excitement anymore; it's fear.

"He'll get over it," Daniel says.

I sit up straight and shake my head. Fuck, my heart is breaking. "No. I told you I wasn't going to choose between you two. This is only happening if we're all on the same page."

Daniel pulls away from me. The frustration is evident on his face as a deep crease has formed between his eyebrows. "God, you're killing me!"

"You guys are best friends. That's not something to take lightly. I refuse to be responsible for fucking that up," I say.

The ache in my lower abdomen is real. I'm so painfully horny, it's nearly impossible to ignore. If it wasn't for the distinct feeling of my heart being torn in half. Someone has to intervene. I have to make this right.

"I'm going to talk to him. Get him back. Maybe we can still fix this."

Daniel nods. I reach for his big fleshy face and lean in for a quick kiss. He reacts primally, with his whole body tensing up, begging for release. His reaction soothes me, but only slightly.

"I'm not giving up this easily," I promise him.

He groans into my mouth. "Hurry. I don't know how long I'll be able to last."

"Don't go anywhere, okay? Please."

"I'll be right here," he says, while taking one of my throw cushions and white-knuckling it in his lap.

I quickly get off the bed and rush out of the room. Where did he go? The door to Josh's room is closed, which is unusual. I knock twice, but he doesn't respond immediately.

"Josh, come on. Let's talk!"

"Nah, I'm good."

"Please, please, please. Let me in," I beg, resting my forehead against the wood.

"It's not locked," he says.

I turn the handle, overcome with trepidation about what I'm walking into. There he is, sitting on his bed with his head in his hands. I take a few steps in his direction but nerves stop me in my tracks.

"What happened, Josh?"

He shrugs. "Look. This is all really big of you, but you really don't have to do all this."

What's he talking about? "What?"

He looks up. His eyes are watery. I can't tell if he's angry or sad. "It's obvious what's going on. Just admit it. Make this easier on everyone."

I take another step forward and rest my hand on his shoulder. Oh, it stings so badly knowing he's upset with me.

"I'm not sure what I did wrong," I whisper. "Everything seemed to be going so well, and then…"

He makes a face and points at the door. "I can see how you look at him. I'm not stupid!"

I open my mouth, but I'm not sure yet what to say, so I close it again.

"This isn't your problem, okay? Just… I'll handle it," he says. "You don't have to pretend anymore."

"I'm not pretending!" I counter. God, is that what he thinks? That I'm trying to fool him? My sweet, darling, Josh. For such a big man, he's really rather fragile. I should have known better. He really can be a big softy sometimes.

I put my arms around him and pull him into me. He's so tense, but he does yield eventually.

"I swear to you. On my life. I'm not pretending. I love you, Josh." I melt against him and bury my face in his hair.

A deep sigh shudders through his broad shoulders. I hold him even tighter and caress his fleshy back.

"Please, baby, don't doubt me. I can't see you hurting like this!" I plead.

He keeps on breathing funnily like that. Is he crying? Before I know it, my own eyes start to well up.

"I love you, Josh," I say again.

"I love you," he whispers. "But I can't-"

"You're jealous."

He pulls back and shakes his head while finally looking up at me. "No. Daniel is like a brother to me. I wish for you two to be happy; you deserve it."

"But I won't be happy. Because I won't have you," I complain through my tears.

God, I sound selfish. But it's how I feel.

"Liar."

"You're the sweetest guy I've ever met. You make me laugh. You take care of me; always there for me when I'm feeling down. I need to just look into your eyes and immediately all seems right in the world again. What would I ever do without you?" I ask.

He pulls his eyebrows together and stares up at me.

"I've loved you from the moment we first met," I whisper, caressing the side of his face. Most of all, I love how utterly handsome he is without realising it. But I worry it would be weird to confess that too right now.

He frowns and shakes his head in disbelief. "What about Daniel?"

"God, I love him too. I love how he sings in the shower, and watches stupid reality shows in his room when he thinks nobody's paying attention. I love his optimism and how ridiculously competitive he gets while playing Xbox."

Josh chuckles through his tears. "Yeah, he does do that, you're right."

"You're both utterly perfect in your own way. How could I possibly choose one over the other?" I ask. "I just need you to be totally honest with me about how *you* feel about all of this. I need to know what you're thinking."

"It's just. I saw how he kissed you. Completely at ease and confident. He's so much better at all this stuff. He knows what he's doing. He'll take care of you the way you deserve," Josh whispers. "I'll just get in the way."

I shake my head. "No. I refuse to go back in there with him, if you're not with me too."

There's a loaded silence between us. The awkwardness is growing by the second.

"I'm terrified of disappointing you," Josh mumbles at last.

"You couldn't possibly. I just want to make you happy," I say. "I've always wanted to make the two of you happy, don't you see?"

"I'm happy just seeing your face every morning," he

says.

"Aw!"

He knows just what to say to melt my heart. He presses his lips together and looks into my eyes, which makes me feel even weaker in the knees. For a split second, he glances downwards and holds his breath. And then I realise this whole time I've been standing there topless in front of him.

"What if you saw me like this every morning?" I whisper. "What if you woke up next to me like this?"

He exhales loudly and shakes his head. "I wouldn't know what to do with myself."

"I do."

Josh looks up at me again and I seize the moment, cupping his fat cheeks in my hand and kissing him like my life depends on it.

"Baby, I can't do this without you," I beg, before dipping my tongue into his mouth and finding his already there, waiting for me. "I crave your touch. Your lips. I want you so badly."

"I don't know- I've never-" he protests.

It dawns on me what he's trying to say. I pull away again and rest my hands on his chest.

"May I touch you? Help you relieve some of this tension?" I nod down at his crotch.

He's sweating profusely. It's obvious against the red blush on his cheeks. His hands grab onto the mattress on either side of him and clamp down.

"You don't have to do this," he stammers.

"I know. But I want to, so badly. Let me make you

feel good. May I?"

He nods ever so briefly, and I fall down onto my knees between his legs. When I slip my fingers into the waistband of his shorts, I realise just how little slack the elastic has. The only reason the shorts still fit is because his body is so squishy, his flesh simply made way for them. He lifts up and helps me take them down to his ankles. That's when I realise he wasn't wearing any underwear underneath. My God, he's beautiful.

His impressive manhood springs forward from the plush flesh of his belly and inner thighs, and points right at me.

"Wow, you're so hard," I whisper. I had wanted to do this with the both of them together. But I think this is an exception worth making. Josh's fragile self-esteem needs the TLC I'm about to offer.

He shudders and groans when I wrap my fingers around his shaft and squeeze down.

"You're gorgeous, you know that?" I say. "Even better than in my dreams."

Josh's right hand ends up in my hair, at first caressing it, but then just freezing in place. He's so tense. He'll feel so much better once I'm done with him.

I dive in for my very first taste and take as much of his beautiful cock into my mouth as I can.

He grinds his hips in my direction. Uncoordinated. Out of control.

I suck him off in long, steady movements. Savouring the salty taste of his precum. Marvelling at how rock hard he has grown for me already.

He lets out a moan every time I go back in, sucking hard on the head of his cock, making sure I fit my tongue around it nicely for extra friction.

"Oh fuck," he grunts, while tightening his grip on my hair. "I can't-"

I speed up, bobbing my head up and down on his glorious thick cock. I caress his inner thighs, squeezing them and marvelling at just how squishy they are, before moving onto his balls. They're so tight; so full and ready to unload. He groans loudly, and shoves my face down against his cock, forcing me to take his full length into my mouth.

It makes my eyes water, but I do my best to stay calm as he shoots a hot load of cum down the back of my throat. His grip on me loosens and he starts to breathe again. Desperate, short panting breaths.

"I'm sorry. I'm so sorry," he whispers.

I carry on sucking him, making sure I get every last drop of jizz out of him while he tries to recover. Then I pull away and look up at his spent face.

"Josh, you're amazing. I can't wait to find out what you'll feel like inside of me. I want you to do it first, okay?"

He whimpers and reaches for my hand. I get up in front of him and wrap my arms around him, soothing his tired body as he recovers from that very first, very rushed orgasm. I hope he'll be ready to go again soon, because I'm far from satisfied yet.

"I love you so much it hurts," he says. "I never thought- Fuck, I don't deserve any of this."

"Baby, you deserve so much more. But all I have to offer between the two of you is me."

A knock on the door behind us interrupts.

"Come in, Dan," I say.

Josh tenses in my embrace, but doesn't protest. I turn my head and see Daniel standing there, still shirtless. Still rocking shorts-full of big black cock for me.

"Umm… you guys okay?" Daniel asks.

I smile at him, then plant a kiss in Josh's hair before loosening my hold on his shoulders. "We are now. Aren't we?"

"Uhh, yeah," Josh mumbles. "I'm good."

"Let's go back to my room?" I suggest. "Together."

When Josh gets up off the edge of the bed, I spot Daniel staring at his naked crotch. He must be wondering what he almost walked in on. For fear of having to deal with another meltdown, I decide to get the original plan back on track. If I can satisfy both of them, they won't have any energy left to be jealous.

"Shorts off," I tell him. Then I tug at the edge of Josh's T-shirt. "And you, shirt off! Let's go!"

I walk off ahead of the two of them, wiggling out of my bikini bottoms as I do so. I glance back once while heading out the door. They're both fumbling with their clothes, before stumbling along behind me. The sight of the two of them, gloriously naked, makes me smile.

Back in my room, I position myself in the centre of the bed again and wait for Josh and Daniel to join me; one on either side, like before.

Now I can finally appreciate the size of Daniel's tool as well. How on earth did he manage to keep this hidden in those shorts?

"Wow, is this all for me?" I coo, while grabbing a handful of balls with my right hand.

He groans desperately. It's obvious that the long wait has been hard on him.

Josh is a bit more relaxed now thanks to that blowjob. But he still is having a tough time knowing just what to look at. My tits, or the neat triangle of hair revealed by my lack of panties. I spread wide and gesture at him to get in between my thighs. He looks eager to return the favour. His eyes widen as he cups his hand over my wet pussy. I smile and bite my bottom lip. "Oh yeah, touch me there."

Meanwhile, I start pumping Daniel's big black cock and look up at his handsome face. He's so close already as well. At this rate, this threesome might just end before it gets going properly.

I let go of his dick and start caressing his thick body instead. He's fat alright, but his flesh is firm under my touch. Plump man boobs, not as big as Josh's, sit at the top of the big, round bulge of his belly. I fondle and squeeze my way around his torso. It's perfect.

"I love this," I whisper. "Big sexy man."

He lies down next to me and wraps his arm around my waist, grinding his crotch into my thigh and moaning into the side of my neck. I reach down and grab his shaft, hard.

"You've got to choose," I say.

Daniel nibbles on my earlobe. "Choose what?"

"Do you want to cum like this, or in my mouth?"

He groans loudly and bucks his hips into me, forcing his cock into my closed fist.

"You're too much!"

"Get up, I want to drink your cum."

Although he's panting already, and desperate to finish himself off in my hand, he does make an effort to get up onto his knees and position himself beside me.

Josh helps me onto my side and caresses my ass before pressing two fingers into my dripping cunt from the back. I lean up to be able to look at him.

His expression is one of intense focus. Little drops of sweat have collected on his brow. I smile at him and he smiles back. Finally. We're on the same page. He rubs my folds with renewed purpose, before finally dipping one of his fingers inside my tight little cunt.

"Oh God, yes, keep doing that!" I cry out.

Daniel, not one to be left out, starts jacking off in front of my face. I lean up onto my elbow and close my lips around the head of his cock for the first time. He too tastes amazing. I swirl my tongue around the tip, then steady myself against his thigh and try to take his whole length into me. It's awkward, while being on my side, so I turn around onto my tummy and start sucking him off more easily.

My mouth is full of glorious dick for the second time in fifteen minutes. These boys are bringing out my inner slut like no one ever has before!

Josh grabs my hips and drags me across his lap, all

while continuing to finger me from behind. His other hand is kneading my ass, cupping it, squeezing it, jiggling it and even spanking it a few times. Whatever he's doing, it's amazing.

I understood what he was trying to say in his room; that today is his first time with a girl, but I couldn't tell from his actions now. He's a new man now. Reborn with one purpose in life: to tease my cunt towards the release I crave so much.

I feel dirty, and powerful, and depraved. I'm ecstatic. Like this is what I was always meant to do. This is worth living for. If it'll keep them happy, I'll be their fuck toy forever.

Daniel is getting painfully close. I can tell from his breathing; or lack thereof. I can feel the tension grow in his thighs and in his balls. I try to bob up and down as fast as I can on him. To give him a mouthfuck dreams are made of.

He's leaning back now, allowing me full control. As though he knows that's what I crave the most. When he cums, I want it to be my achievement and mine alone.

With every downward stroke of my mouth, his belly shudders beautifully above me. I can't see his face, but I can imagine it. The ecstasy he feels, it's like I can feel it too. Of course, that's mostly Josh's doing… By now he's added a second finger to the party, much to my delight.

And what's even better is, underneath me, in his lap, there's something else that's eager to join. I'm surprised at how fast he's been able to recover. Awkward virgin no more; Josh is all man and I'm ready for him to take what's his. I hope he remembers what I told him. That I want him to fuck me first.

I wiggle free from his grasp and get onto my knees. As he withdraws his fingers from my pussy, a sense of loss fills me that must be filled immediately. I gesture at him to get into position behind me.

He struggles onto his knees as well now, spreads me wide from behind and-

"Oh God!" I cry out into Daniel's cock, when Josh's fat erection pushes its way inside my pussy, stretching me wider than I recall ever being stretched. It has been a while. Much too long. I've been saving myself for these two, and as a result, I'm so very tight it's almost like I'm a virgin myself again.

Daniel bucks his hips underneath my face, forcing my attention back on him again. I suck him with renewed purpose. Harder than before. Faster.

He grits his teeth and groans loudly. His body freezes underneath me, rigid and immovable except for one part of him: his cock squirms and pulsates in between my lips. A hot load of cum gets shot into my throat. It's so much, I'm finding it hard to swallow it all in one go.

"Oh, Lucy!" Daniel cries. "Oh God, stop!"

But I don't. I can't. I lick him clean and marvel at the intensity of his release.

Meanwhile, Josh is getting the hang of doggy style behind me. With a firm grip on my hips, he's slamming into me, fucking me like I've never been fucked before.

Faster and faster, he makes my cunt burn with anticipation. Because I will only be able to keep up for so long, before the inevitable happens.

"Please Josh," I whimper. "Please give it to me good!"

He does. *Smack, smack, smack,* his flesh pounds into me. It's amazing just how powerful it feels when a man can bring some heft into the bedroom.

This is it. This is what I've been yearning for all these months! This is my reward for stuffing the two of them like pigs; making them gain for me, grow for me, and apparently, lust after me all at the same time. I'm done for. I have been conquered.

All the tension I've carried in my lower abdomen all afternoon, it releases and erupts. I'm overcome with pleasure; helpless and yet all-powerful as my cunt contracts around Josh's beautiful cock. Even my body doesn't want to let him go now that I've finally got him.

He shudders to a halt, balls-deep inside of me, overwhelmed by his own orgasm. I'm impressed at just how much cum the boy has got to give to me.

"Lucy, I love you-" he cries out.

I'm speechless. A mess of emotions; of sensations. My skin tingles all over; my limbs might as well be made of lead.

Tears are streaming down my face as I raise my head from Daniel's lap. His hands welcome me into a warm embrace, cradling my face, smoothing down my damp hair.

His lips are already waiting to love mine and my

heart overflows yet again.

I knew that this was the right call. Every few minutes I feel like one of them becomes my favourite, only for the other one to catch up and exceed my expectations yet again. I wouldn't even know how to explain it, so I do the only thing I *can* do. Kiss him. I curl up in Daniel's arms and tenderly kiss his lips, smiling into them as I do so.

Josh pulls out of me, leaving me wanting from behind.

But I think we've all deserved a breather, no matter how badly I want to change positions and do it all over again. I push Daniel down onto the bed. He lands on one of my many pillows, and I settle down beside him with my head resting against his shoulder.

Josh is busy wiping our combined juices off his cock with his shorts. He looks at me, as though he can sense my eyes burning into him.

"Please come join us," I whisper, and pat the empty side of the bed next to me.

He does and wraps one arm around me. It feels so warm against my damp skin; I love it.

"That was… wow," Daniel says.

I take a deep breath and close my eyes. A smile creeps over my face.

"Had I known you both felt this way about me… We might have done this sooner," I say.

Josh sighs and nuzzles my hair.

This moment, shared between the three of us, is utterly perfect. Perhaps even more so than the sex that preceded it.

"I meant everything I said. I do love you both," I add.

"Why didn't you say so earlier?" Josh asks.

"I too was worried it would ruin our friendship. You've been the best roommates a girl could ask for."

"And now?" Daniel asks.

"Now I'm hoping you'll be the best boyfriends. Because I'm far from done with the two of you."

Josh inhales sharply and tightens his grip around my waist. "I'll never know what I did to deserve all this."

"Yeah, same," Daniel agrees.

"You didn't have to do anything. Just be yourselves," I say.

"But you're so beautiful. Way out of our league," Daniel says.

I turn my head and smile at him before giving him a peck on the cheek. "You're absolutely perfect, you know that? I wouldn't change a single thing about you."

Then, I turn my head the other way and find Josh already staring at me with those pale blue eyes of his. "And you too. A perfect dream."

It occurs to me that maybe I'd like to feed them some more during the coming months. See what happens once they grow even fatter for me. Let's see. But for the moment, I mean it. They're both absolutely gorgeous the way they are. And I can't believe they're all mine to love.

"Who's hungry for a snack?" I suggest, while raising myself up onto both elbows.

Daniel chuckles. "That sounds like a great idea."

"Sure," Josh agrees.

"And after that, I want to do this all over again. This time I'll be on top," I say.

The mood changes yet again. I look over at Josh, whose stare has intensified, then back at Daniel, who looks equally affected. My beautiful boys. I've awoken a whole new kind of hunger in them, one which I'm determined to satisfy. Every single day, in every possible way we can think of together!

ABOUT THE AUTHOR

Dear Reader,

If you came across me in real life, you'd never guess the kind of filth I like to read and write. Cleverly disguised as a boring office worker, the drudgery of my 9-to-5 only becomes bearable because of my vivid and explicit imagination. I like fat guys and I cannot lie. In my world, bigger (fatter) is always better. It's been that way for as long as I can remember.

Thanks for reading this story, one of hopefully many of my published sexual fantasies. My stories revolve around one common theme: really big men and the women who can't help but lust for them.

Although I like porn just fine, it's nearly impossible to find it in the flavour that I desire. The written word allows me to explore a world of lush excess that mainstream adult entertainment just cannot provide. When I started writing, I soon discovered the beauty of having a catalog of erotica out there to satisfy my own lustful needs. This is a passion project more than a money-grab.

So, first and foremost, my writing is for me. But perhaps there are other women (or even men) out there who share my tastes; my fetishes and fantasies? My fascination with the larger male form, and sexualisation of food (especially overeating). If that sounds like something you'll wank off to, you've come to the right place.

xxx Hedonist

To find out more, check:

- ❖ eXplicitTales.com

www.ingramcontent.com/pod-product-compliance
Lightning Source LLC
Chambersburg PA
CBHW070513170726
48291CB00008B/2730